Dear Parent:
Your child's love of reading starts here!

Every child learns to read in a different way and at his or her own speed. Some go back and forth between reading levels and read favorite books again and again. Others read through each level in order. You can help your young reader improve and become more confident by encouraging his or her own interests and abilities. From books your child reads with you to the first books he or she reads alone, there are I Can Read Books for every stage of reading:

SHARED READING
Basic language, word repetition, and whimsical illustrations, ideal for sharing with your emergent reader

BEGINNING READING
Short sentences, familiar words, and simple concepts for children eager to read on their own

READING WITH HELP
Engaging stories, longer sentences, and language play for developing readers

READING ALONE
Complex plots, challenging vocabulary, and high-interest topics for the independent reader

ADVANCED READING
Short paragraphs, chapters, and exciting themes for the perfect bridge to chapter books

I Can Read Books have introduced children to the joy of reading since 1957. Featuring award-winning authors and illustrators and a fabulous cast of beloved characters, I Can Read Books set the standard for beginning readers.

A lifetime of discovery begins with the magical words **"I Can Read!"**

Visit www.icanread.com for information on enriching your child's reading experience.

THIS IS MY TOWN

BY MERCER MAYER

HarperCollinsPublishers

To the children of Roxbury

Library of Congress catalog card number: 2008923461
ISBN 978-0-06-083550-7 (trade bdg.) — ISBN 978-0-06-083549-1 (pbk.)
11 12 13 LP/WOR 10 9 8 7 6 5 4 3   ❖   First Edition

A Big Tuna Trading Company LLC/J. R. Sansevere Book
www.littlecritter.com

This is my town.
This is where I live.

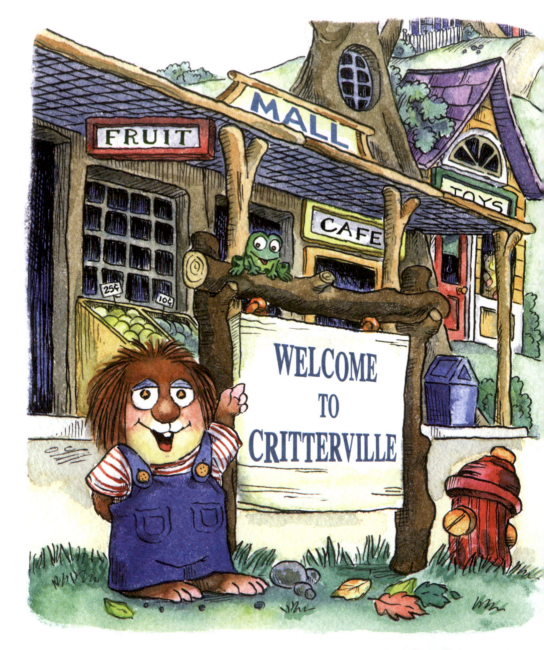

These are the people
in my town.
They live here, too.

This is our post office.

The mail comes in here.

I come here to mail letters.

This is our fire station.

The fire truck lives here.

Oo! Ee! Oo! go the sirens.

When there is a fire,
the firemen go to it.
They put the fire out.

This is our police station.
Police officers work here.

They keep our town safe.

This is our diner.

Sometimes we come
here for lunch. Yum!

This is our town hall.

Our mayor works here.

Sometimes we have parades in our town.

This is our library.

I come here to find

books to read.

During story hour,
the librarian reads to us.

But when story hour is over
we have to be quiet.

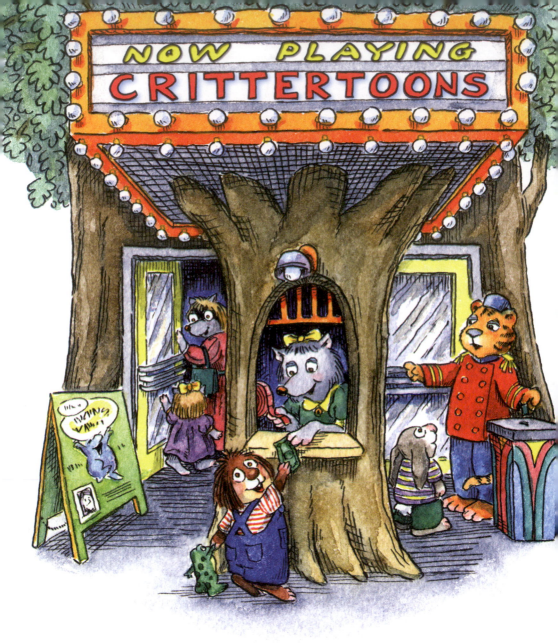

This is our movie theater.

I can buy my own ticket.

I like to get popcorn.

I am always extra careful.

This is our store.

Sometimes Mom and Dad
let me walk here by myself.

This is our school.
My friends and I
are in Miss Kitty's class.

School is fun!

This is our park.

We play football here.

This is our bakery.

It has the best cupcakes.

This is the office
of our town newspaper.
It is a busy place.

Look! Last week
my picture was
in the newspaper.

This is my town.

It is the nicest place

in the whole world.